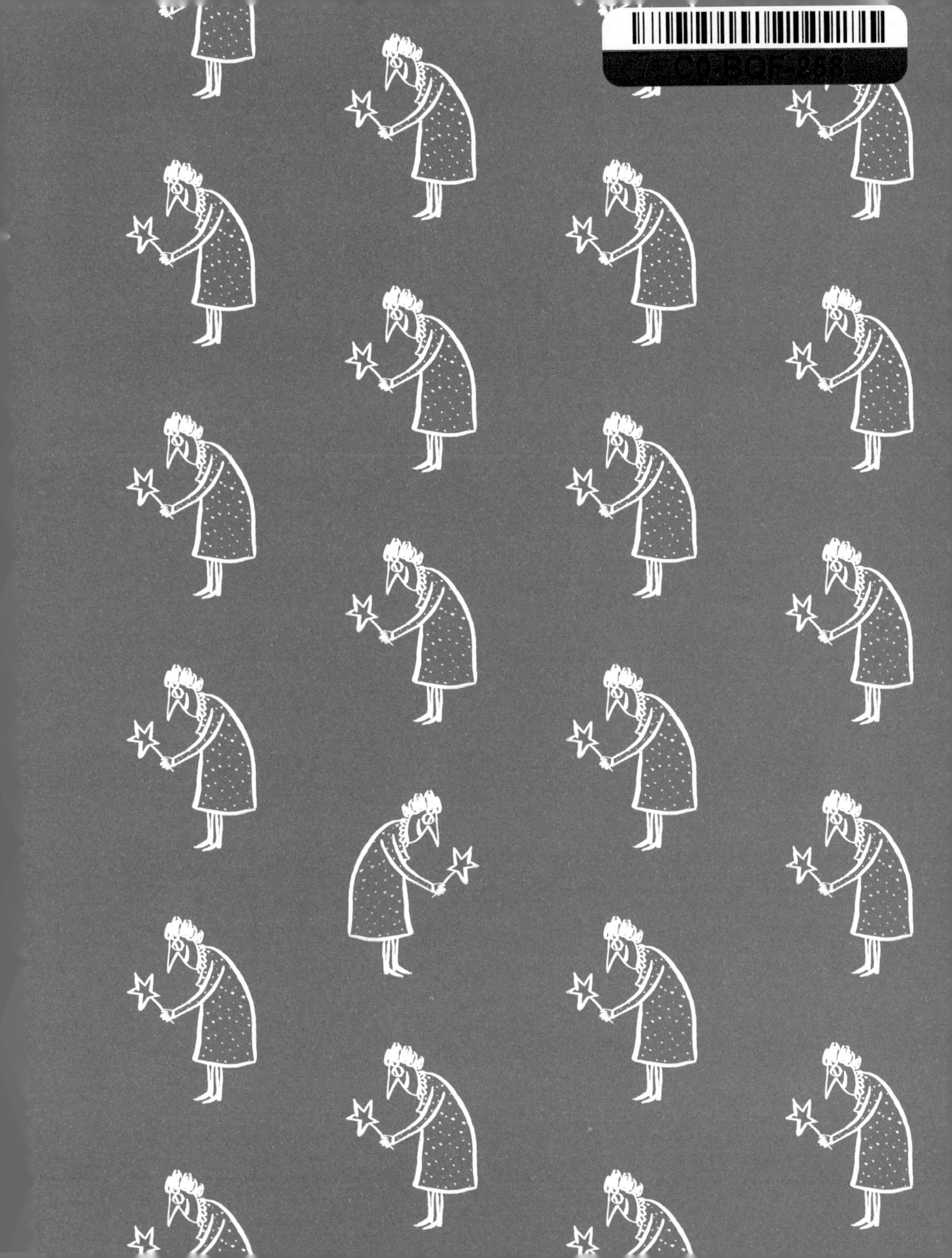

Cinderella

Retold by **michèle marineau**

Illustrated by **mylène pratt**

Tundra Books

Originally published in French as *Cendrillon* by les éditions Les 400 coups, Montreal, 2000
First published in this edition by Tundra Books, Toronto, 2007

English translation copyright © 2007, Tundra Books
Interior illustrations reproduced by permission of les éditions Les 400 coups

Published in Canada by Tundra Books,
75 Sherbourne Street, Toronto, Ontario M5A 2P9

Published in the United States by Tundra Books of Northern New York,
P.O. Box 1030, Plattsburgh, New York 12901

Library of Congress Control Number: 2006909656

Library and Archives Canada Cataloguing in Publication

Marineau, Michèle, 1955-
[Cendrillon. English]
     Cinderella : adaptation of Cendrillon by Charles
Perrault / retold by Michèle Marineau ; illustrated by Mylène Pratt.

Translation of: Cendrillon: d'après Charles Perrault.
For ages 4-7.
ISBN 978-0-88776-825-5

     1. Cinderella (Legendary character)–Juvenile fiction.
I. Pratt, Mylène II. Title. III. Title: Cendrillon. English.

PS8576.A657C4513 2007   jC843'.54   C2006-906072-X

We acknowledge the financial support of the Government of Canada through the
Book Publishing Industry Development Program (BPIDP) and that of the Government of Ontario
through the Ontario Media Development Corporation's Ontario Book Initiative. We further
acknowledge the support of the Canada Council for the Arts and the Ontario Arts Council
for our publishing program.

ONTARIO ARTS COUNCIL
CONSEIL DES ARTS DE L'ONTARIO

Printed in China

1 2 3 4 5 6   12 11 10 09 08 07

To Sophie
— M.M.

To Simone
— M.P.

Cynthia lived with her father in a little house in a big city. They were as happy as can be. Happy, that is, until her father, who had been a widower for many years, fell in love.

One day, he had news, "I'm getting married, my dear! And your new stepmother has two daughters. Isn't that great?"

It wasn't that great. The two daughters cried and carried on all through the wedding ceremony. "Weird," said Cynthia. "Something tells me that life with these two is not going to be fun."

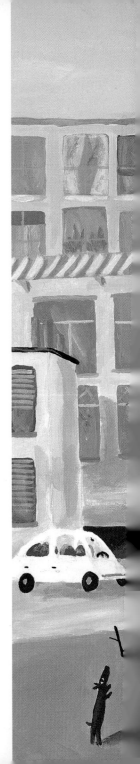

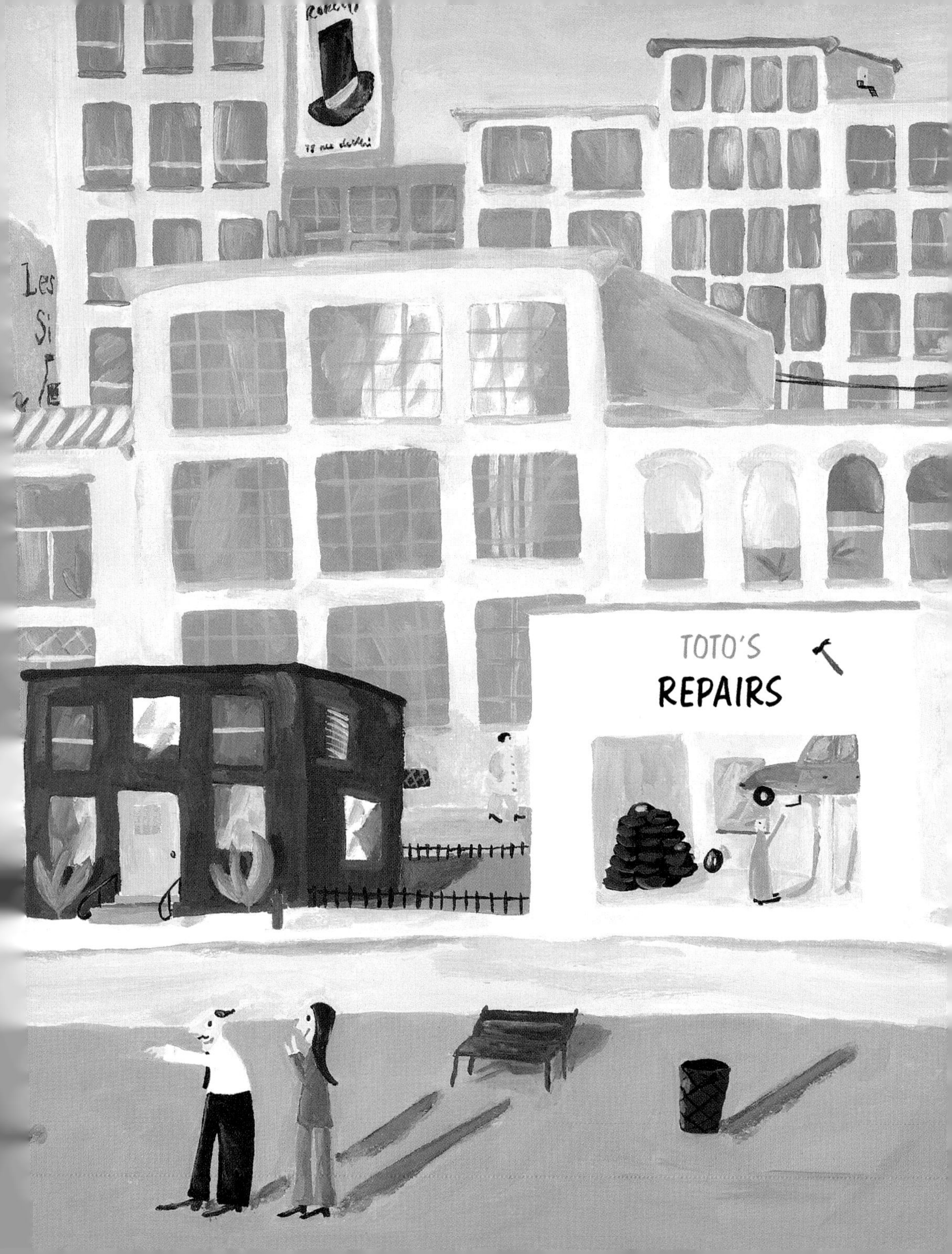

TOTO'S
REPAIRS

She was right. Her stepmother and her two stepsisters were lazy. *Really* lazy. All day long they slept, watched TV, and slept some more while the poor girl cleaned and swept and scrubbed.

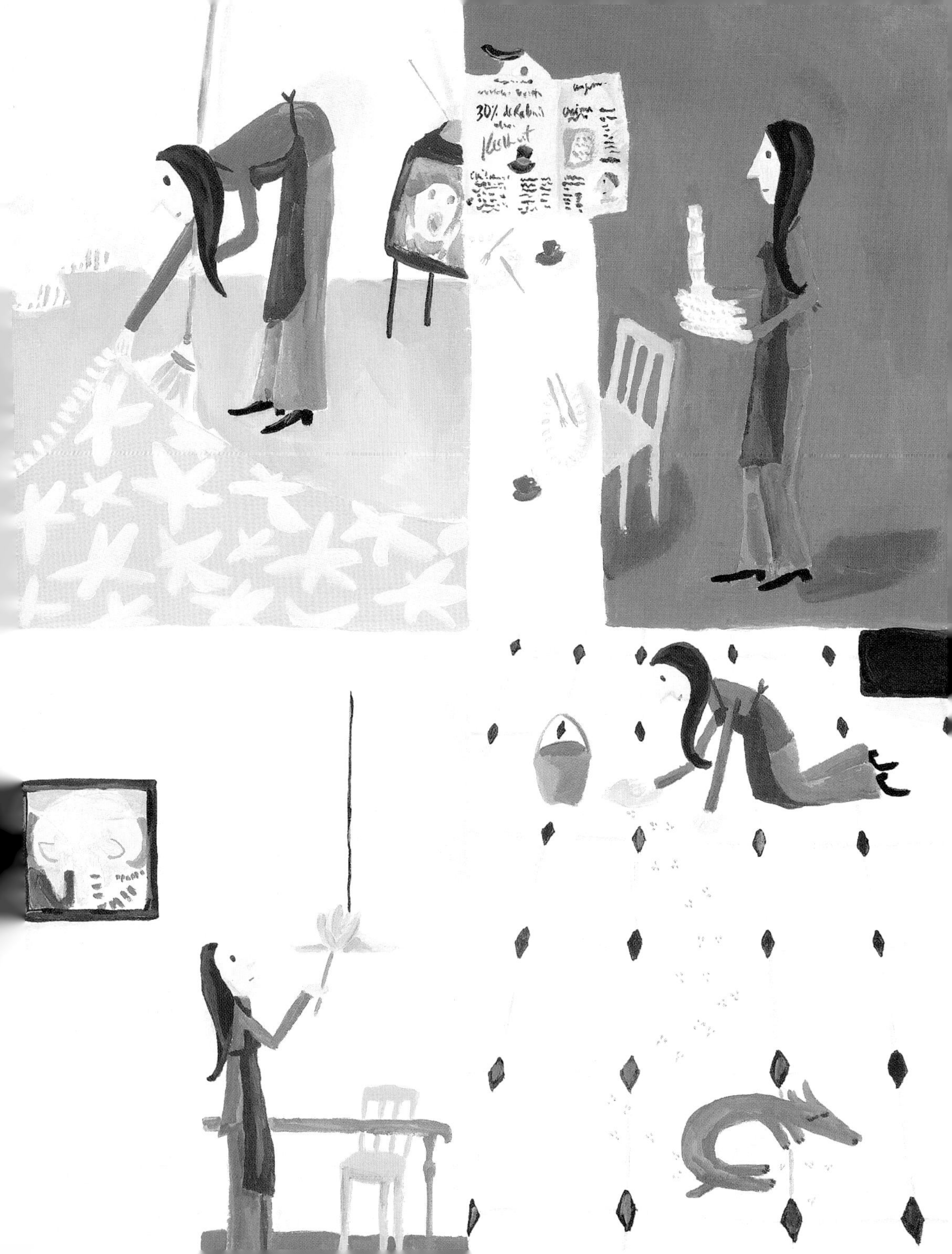
30%

In the evening, tired out, Cynthia curled up in front of the fireplace, with only the cinders to keep her company. And that is how her lazy, yawning half sisters came to call her Cinderella.

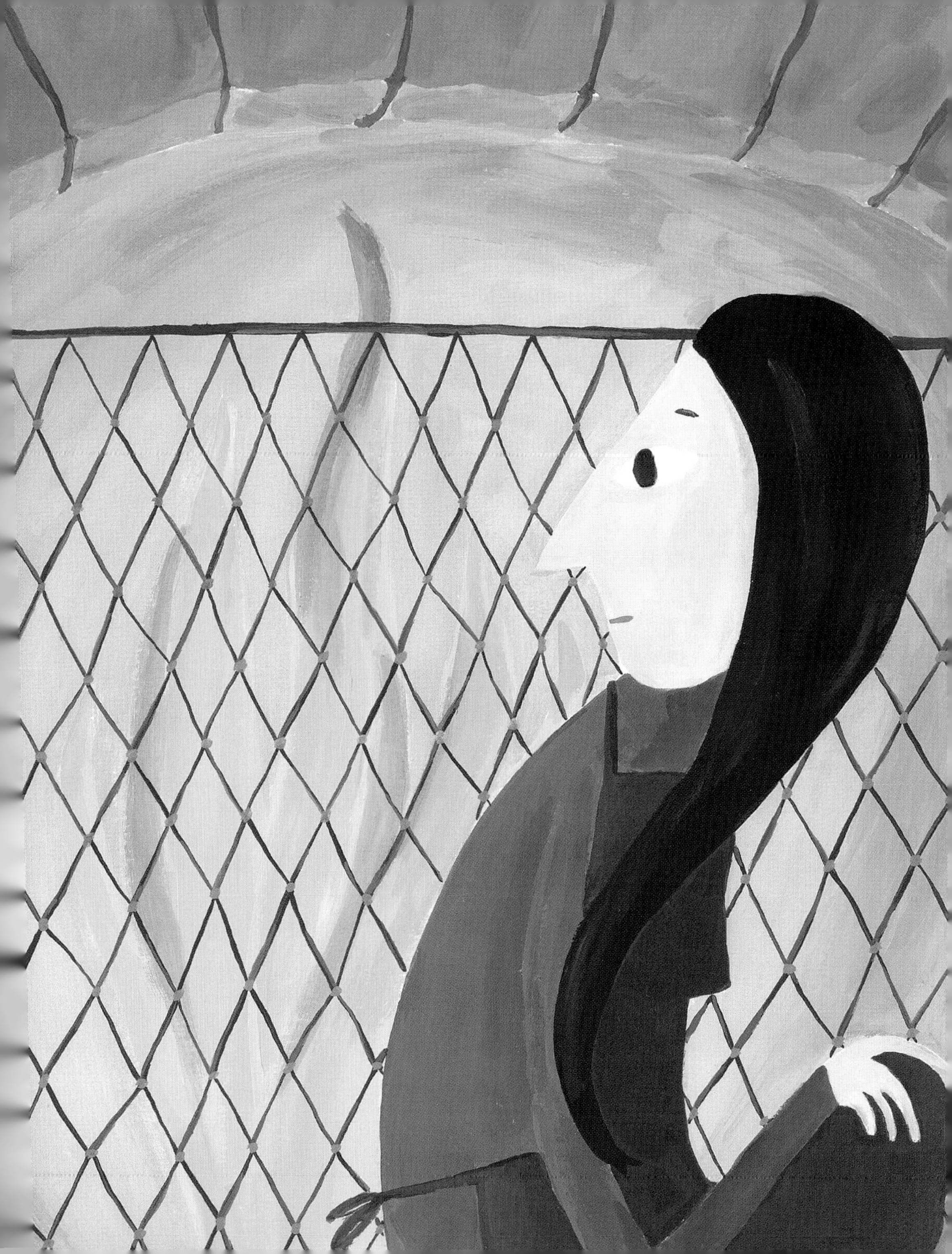

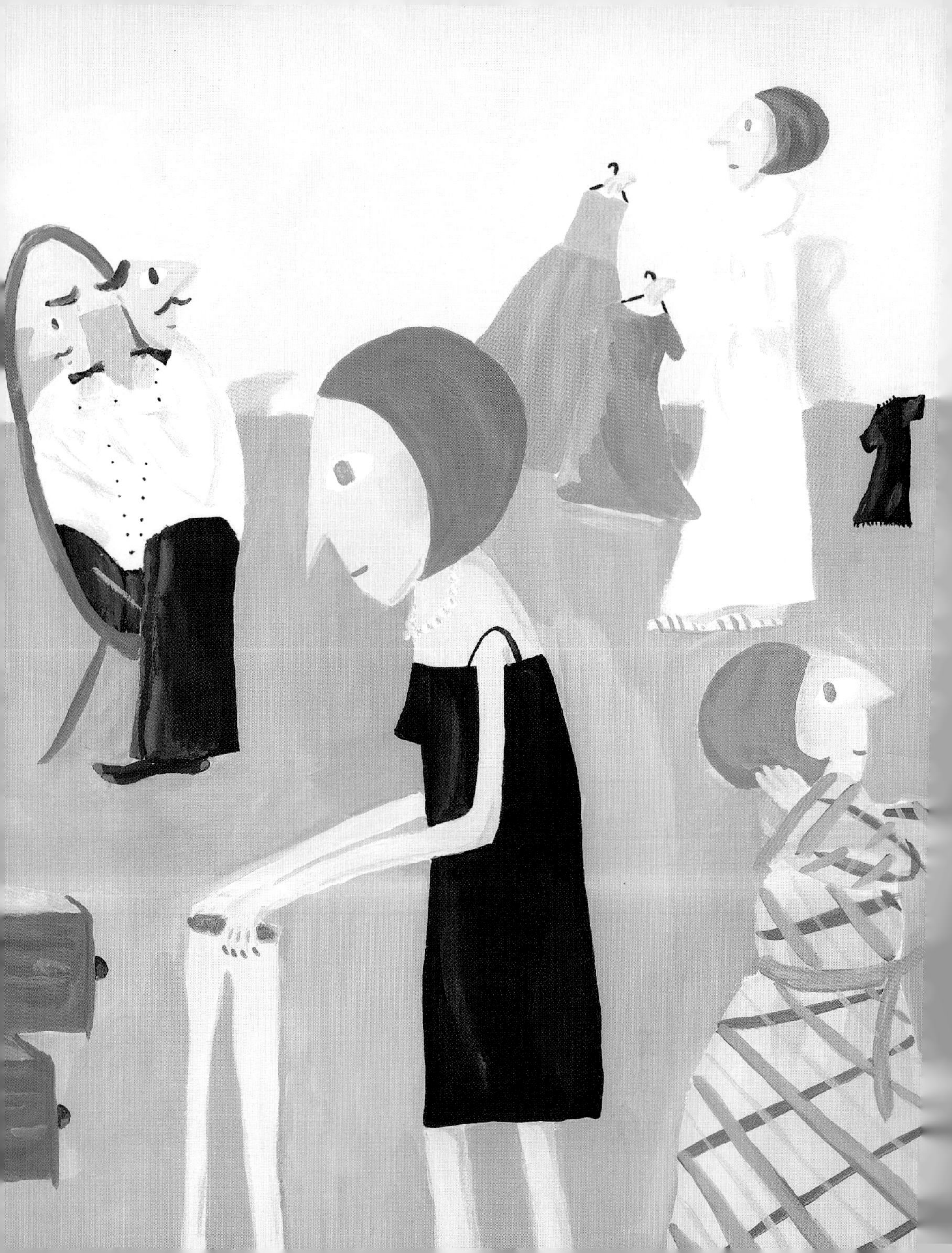

One day, the king announced that he would throw a grand ball, and the whole family was invited. Well, *almost* the whole family.

"Good heavens," said her stepmother, "Cinderella go to the ball? How silly! She has too much to do."

But Cinderella wanted so much to go to the ball. "Is this all there is to my life?" she asked herself quietly, after the others had left. "How can I go on like this?"

"Stop feeling sorry for yourself this instant!" said a stern voice. "You must take charge and change your own life, young lady."

The familiar voice startled Cinderella. It belonged to her fairy godmother. Cinderella saw her so rarely these days that she had forgotten that she even had one.

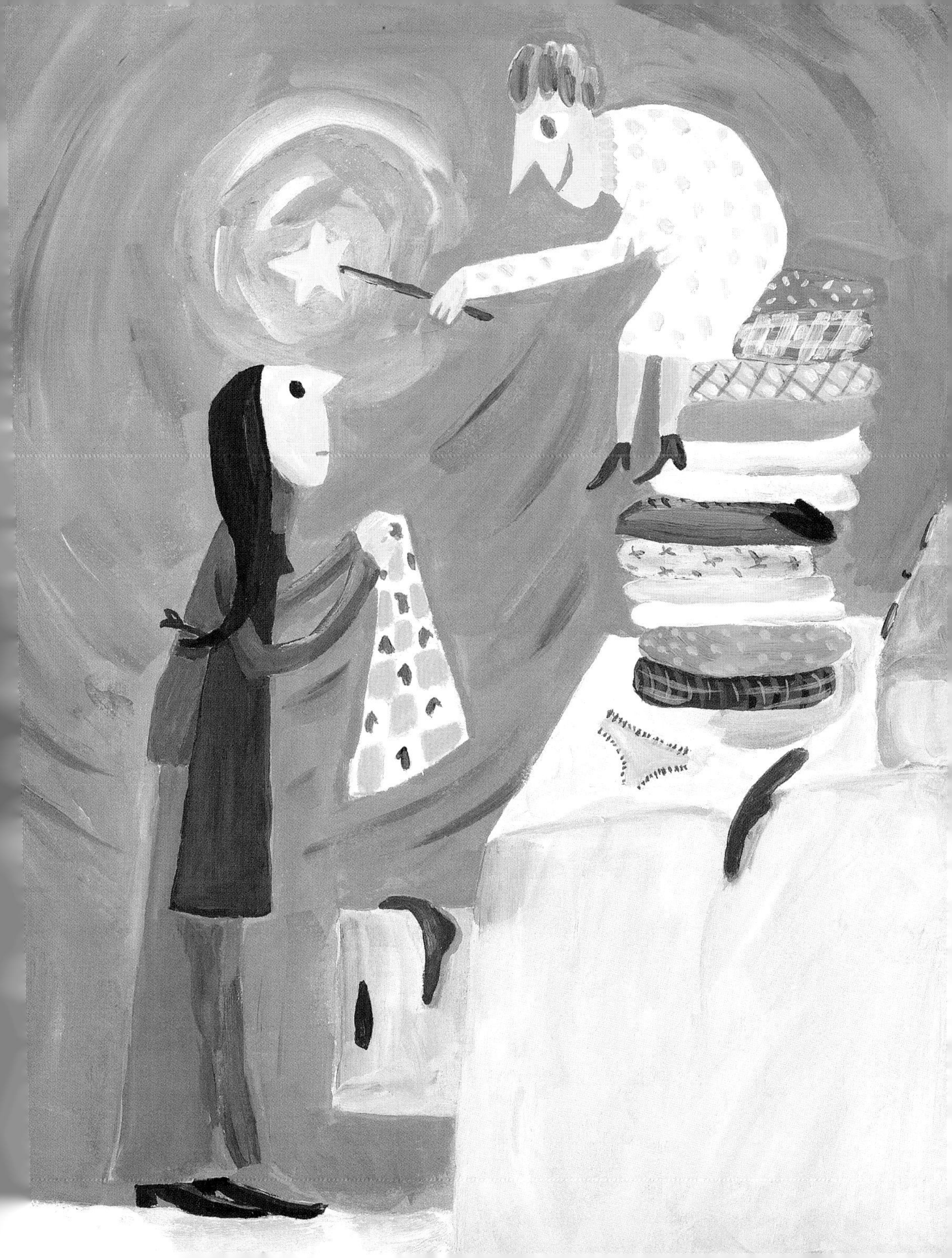

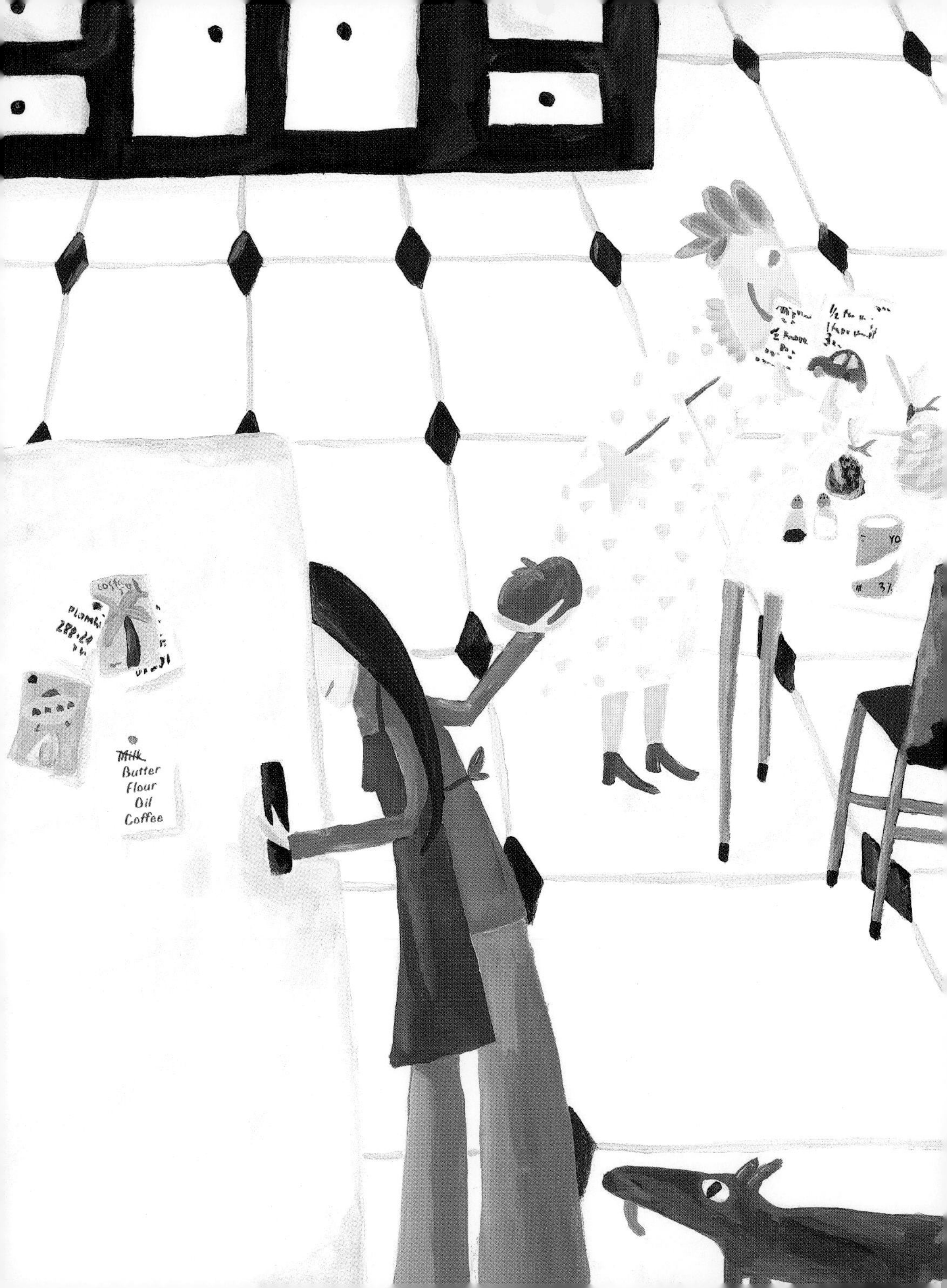
~~Milk~~
Butter
Flour
Oil
Coffee

"If you want to go to the ball," said her fairy godmother, "to the ball you shall go!"

"But how?" asked Cinderella. "I don't have nice clothes or beautiful jewels or a car or. . . "

"Don't forget that I'm a fairy," her fairy godmother replied briskly. "All we need are the right ingredients. *Aha.* Here we have them: a nice ripe tomato, some vanilla yogurt, raisins, and . . . and . . . a dog. With a tap from my magic wand, they should do the trick."

And they did. Everything was perfect.
Cinderella had a bright red car, a
creamy gown, a string of pearls, and
a chauffeur. An unusual chauffeur.
Cinderella could only stare.

"Smile!" ordered her fairy godmother.
"Without a smile, all the other stuff
doesn't count. And remember – above
all – you must return before midnight.
That's when the car will turn back into a
tomato, and the dress, the pearls, the
chauffeur, everything, will vanish."

The fairy godmother had now said all
that she had to say, so she said no more.

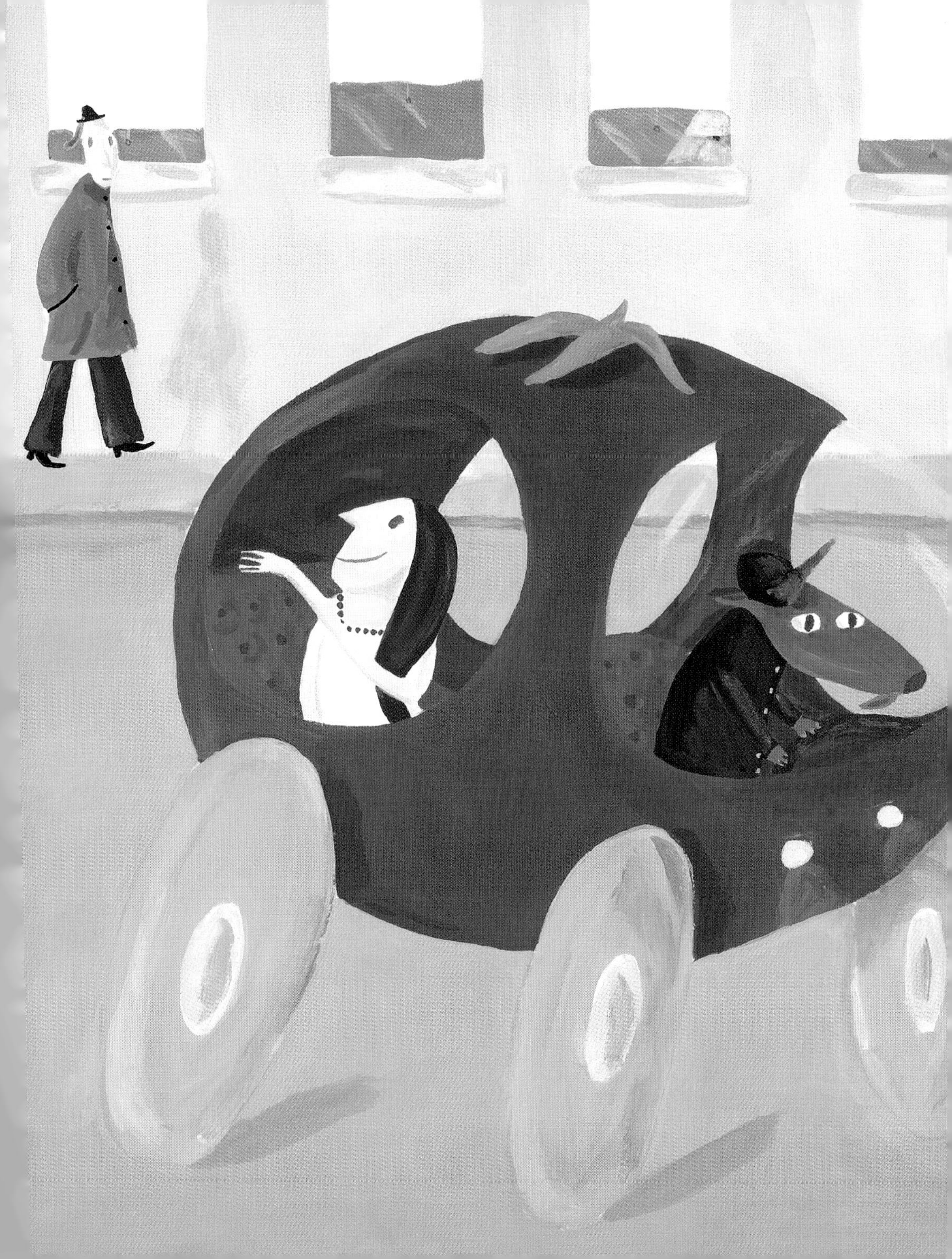

When Cinderella arrived at the ball, everyone turned to stare at the lovely girl in her creamy-silk dress and shimmering pearls. No one recognized her, not even her stepmother and stepsisters.

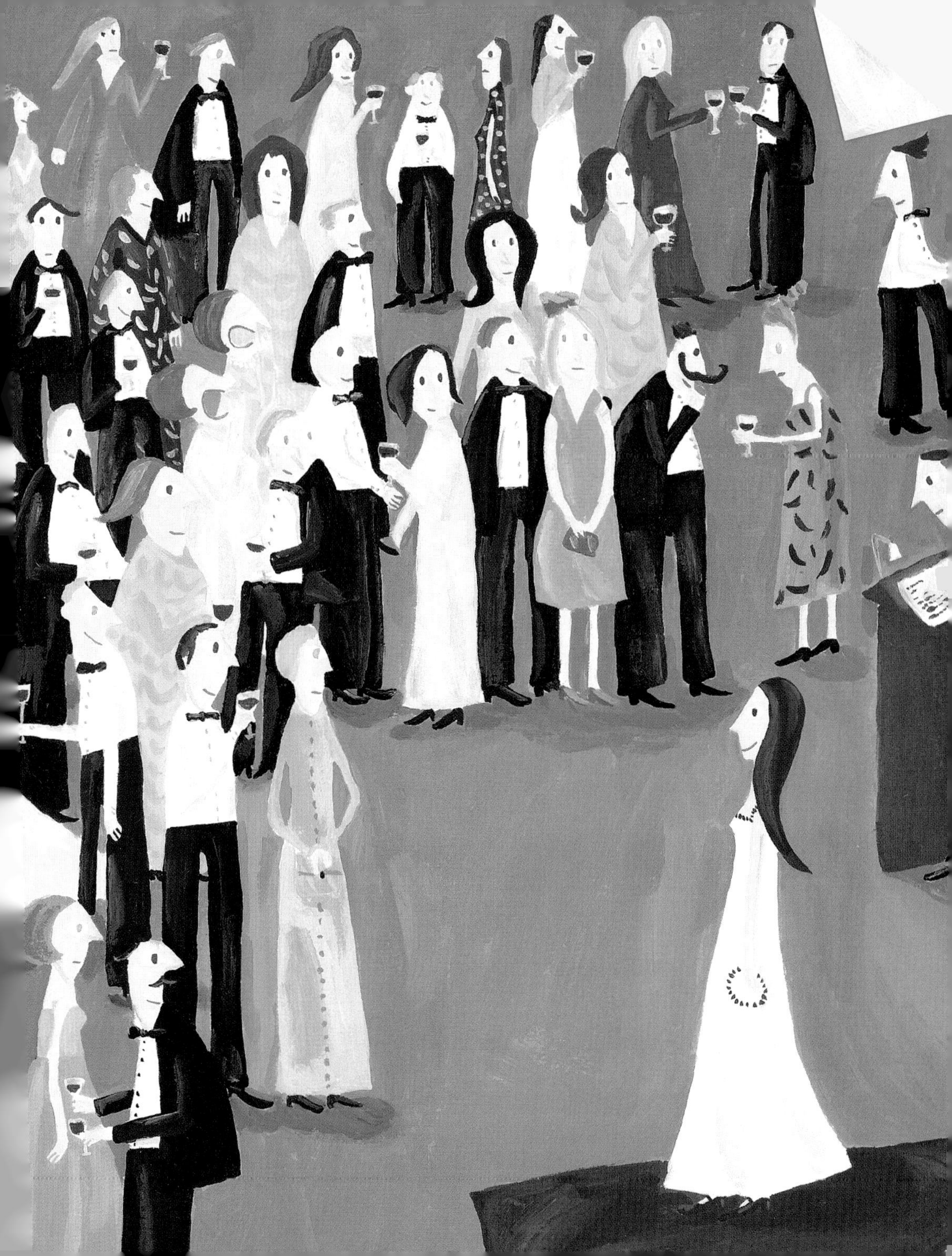

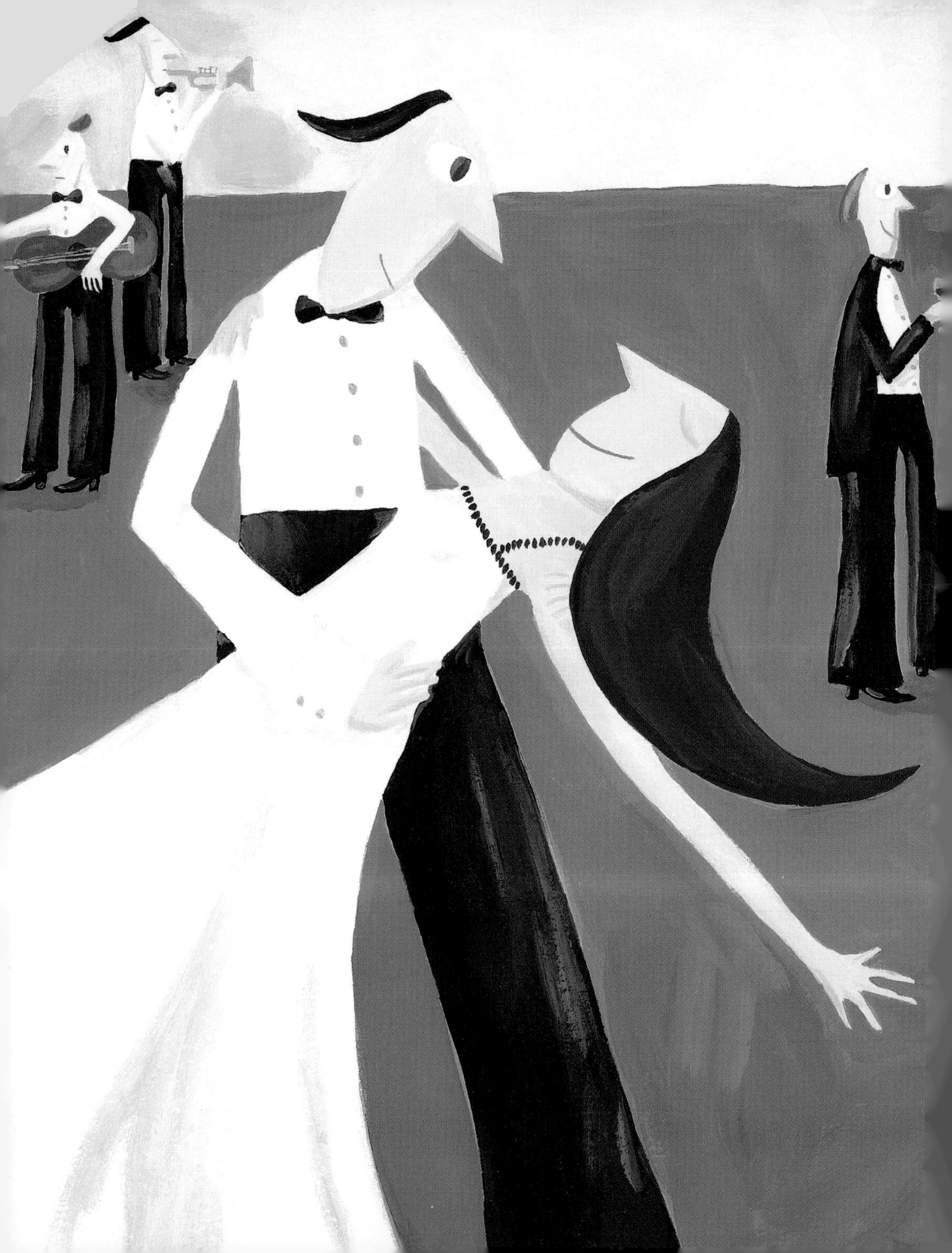

The prince was captivated by the mysterious, beautiful guest. *She is so beautiful!* he
thought. *Such a lovely dress, such eyes, the way
she holds her head! And her smile, such a smile!*
(As it turned out, her fairy godmother
was right about the smile.)

All night long, the prince danced only
with Cinderella.

And Cinderella, lost in the prince's deep brown eyes, danced the night away as though she were in a dream. Until a sudden noise brought her back to reality.

Dong, dong . . . .

"Midnight!" she cried. "I must go." And Cinderella ran so fast that she lost her shoe.

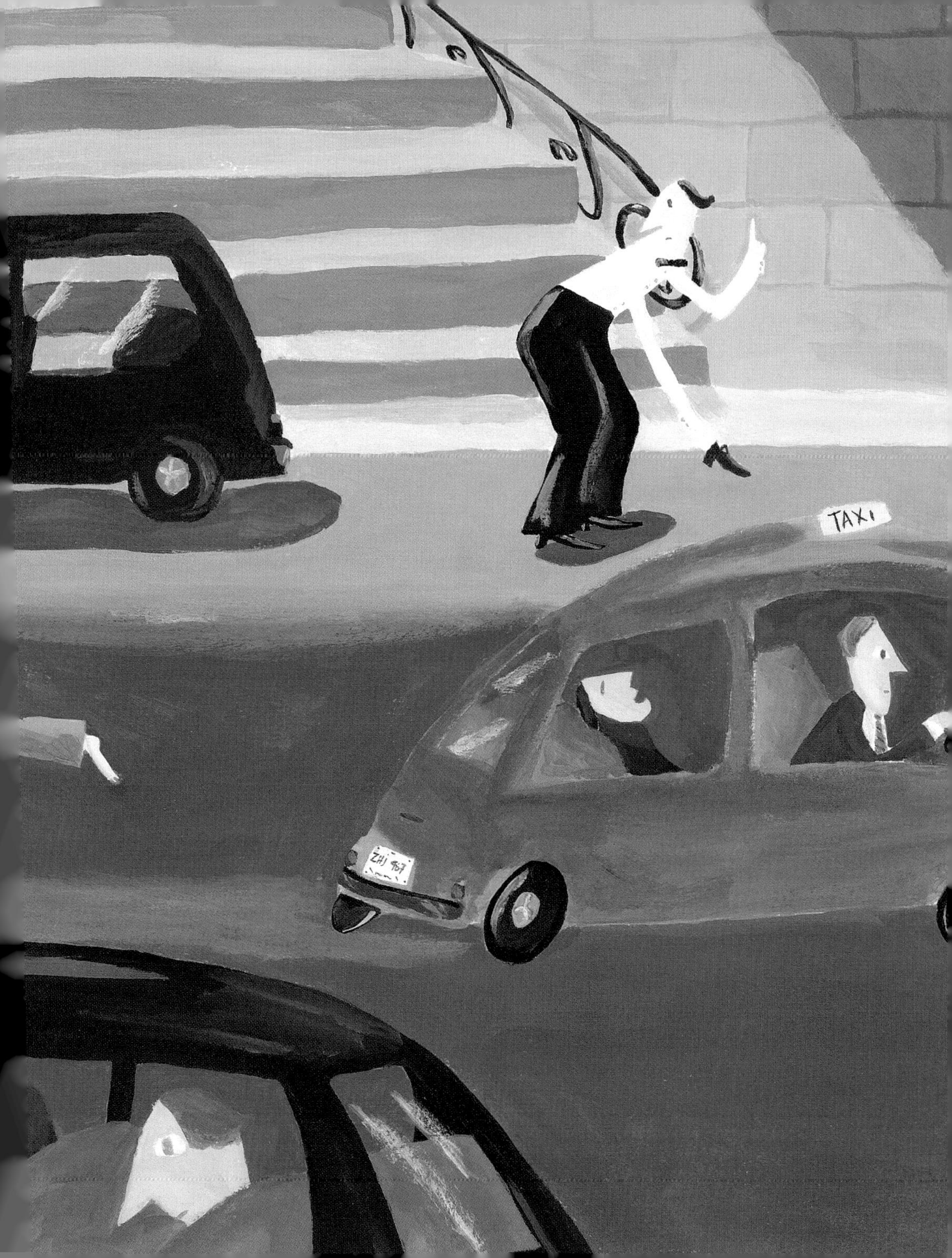
TAXI
ZHJ 967

"Wow!" said Cinderella when she got home. "What a fabulous evening! And, boy, was the prince ever charming!"

The rest of the family arrived not long
after her. "Wow!" said her stepmother and
stepsisters. "What a boring evening! Thank
goodness the prince was charming!"

Not only was the prince charming, he was also persistent — and crazy about the mysterious beauty from the ball.

"Thank goodness I found her shoe. It is as delicate and tiny as she was. Her shoe won't fit anyone else's foot. With a bit of patience, I'm sure I'll find her."

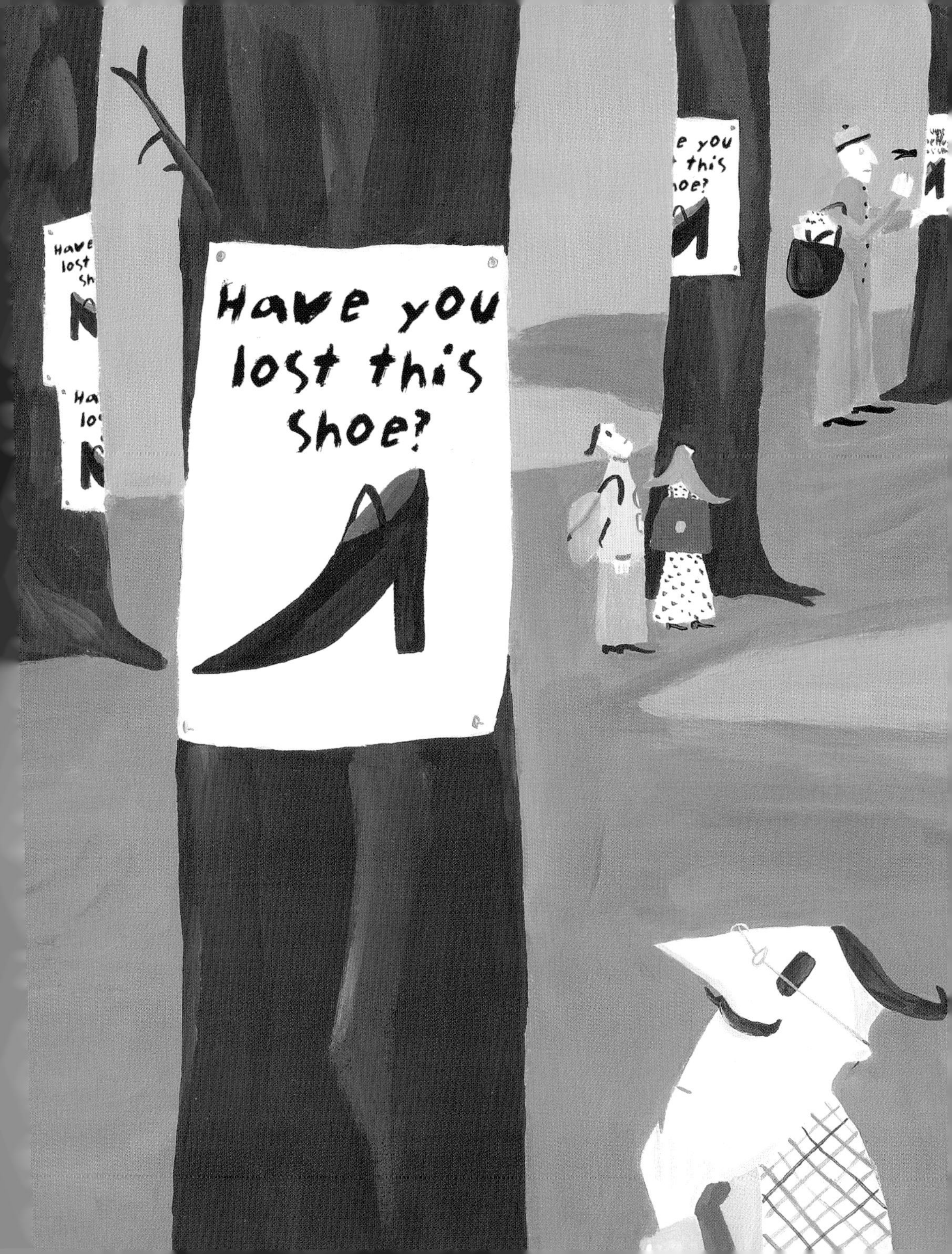
Have you lost this shoe?

The days passed, and the prince tried the shoe on many different feet. He soon grew discouraged. "This is exhausting. All these feet. . . . "

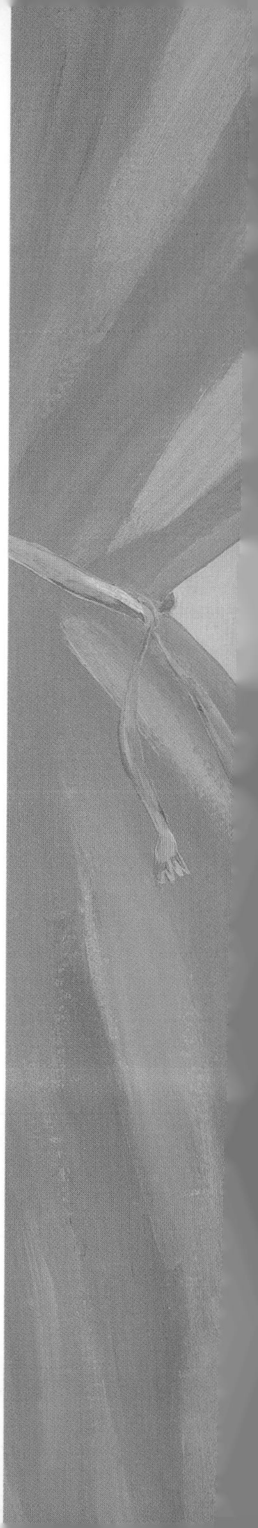

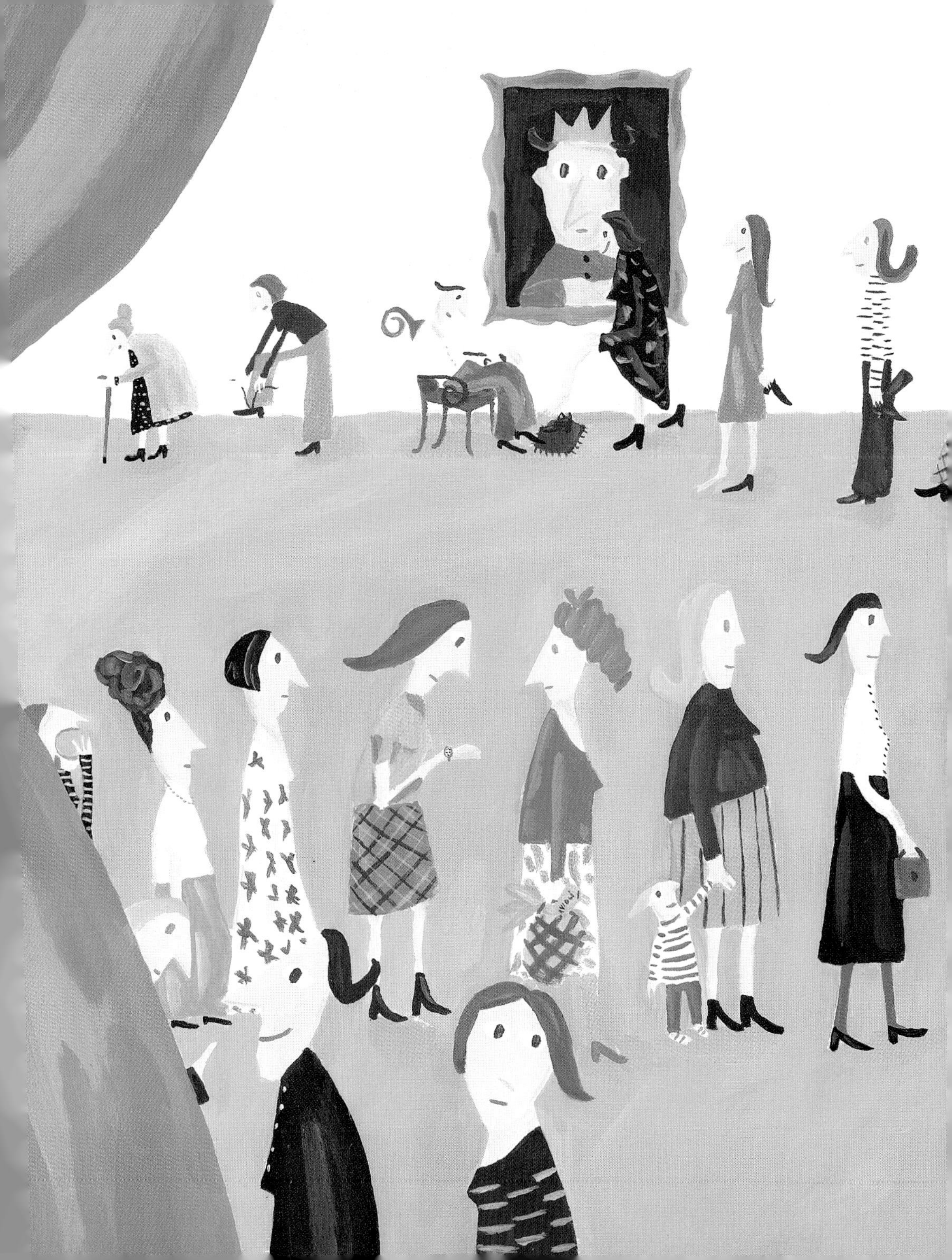

And then one morning, a delicate little foot slid gently into the shoe. The prince looked up and instantly recognized the smile that had won his heart at the ball.

"Oh, my darling, will you marry me?"

How could Cinderella resist those brown eyes, that noble profile, that speckled shirt?

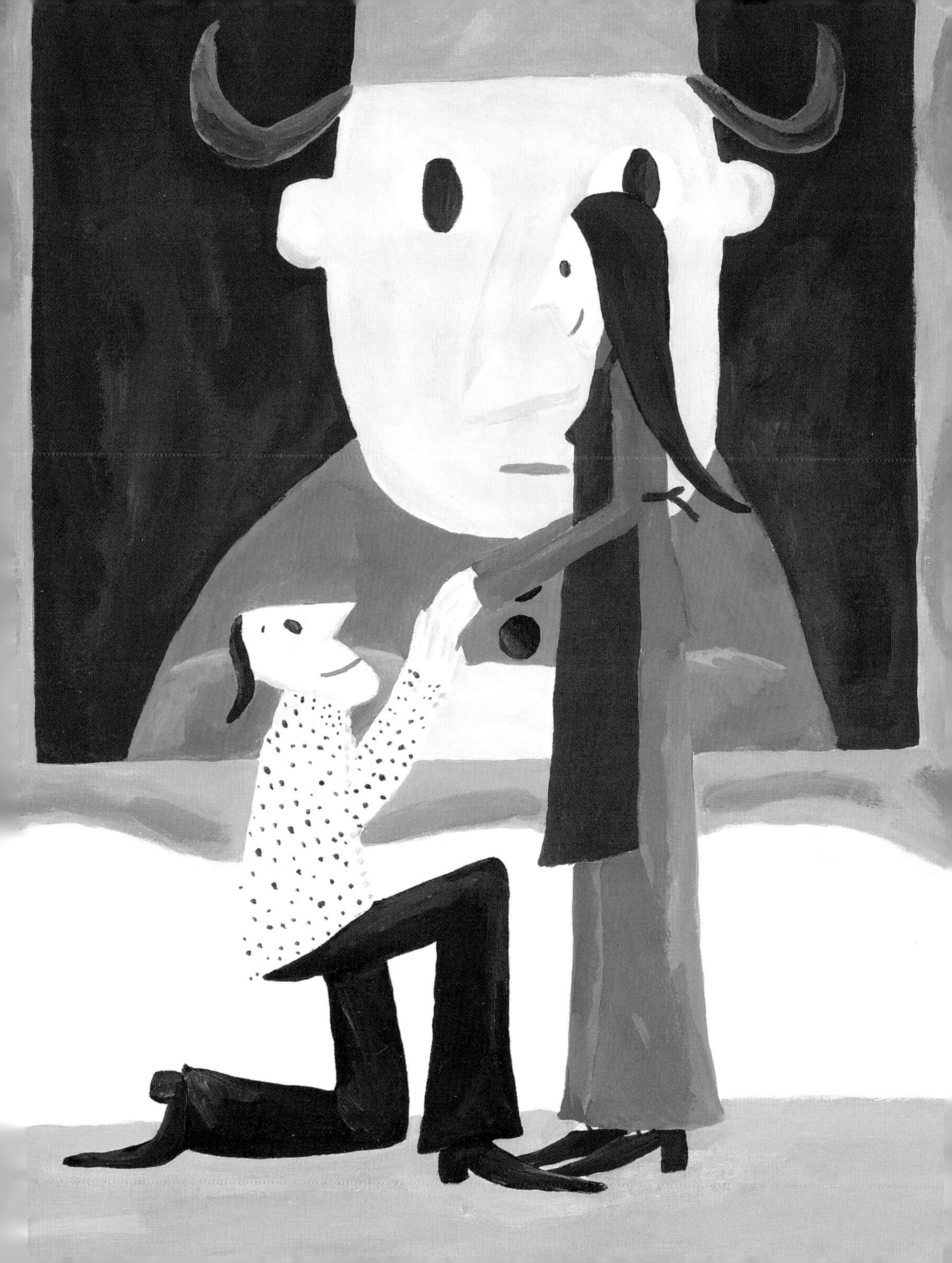

So Cinderella and the prince were married,
and they lived happily ever after, surrounded
by tomatoes, dogs, and lots of children.

The End

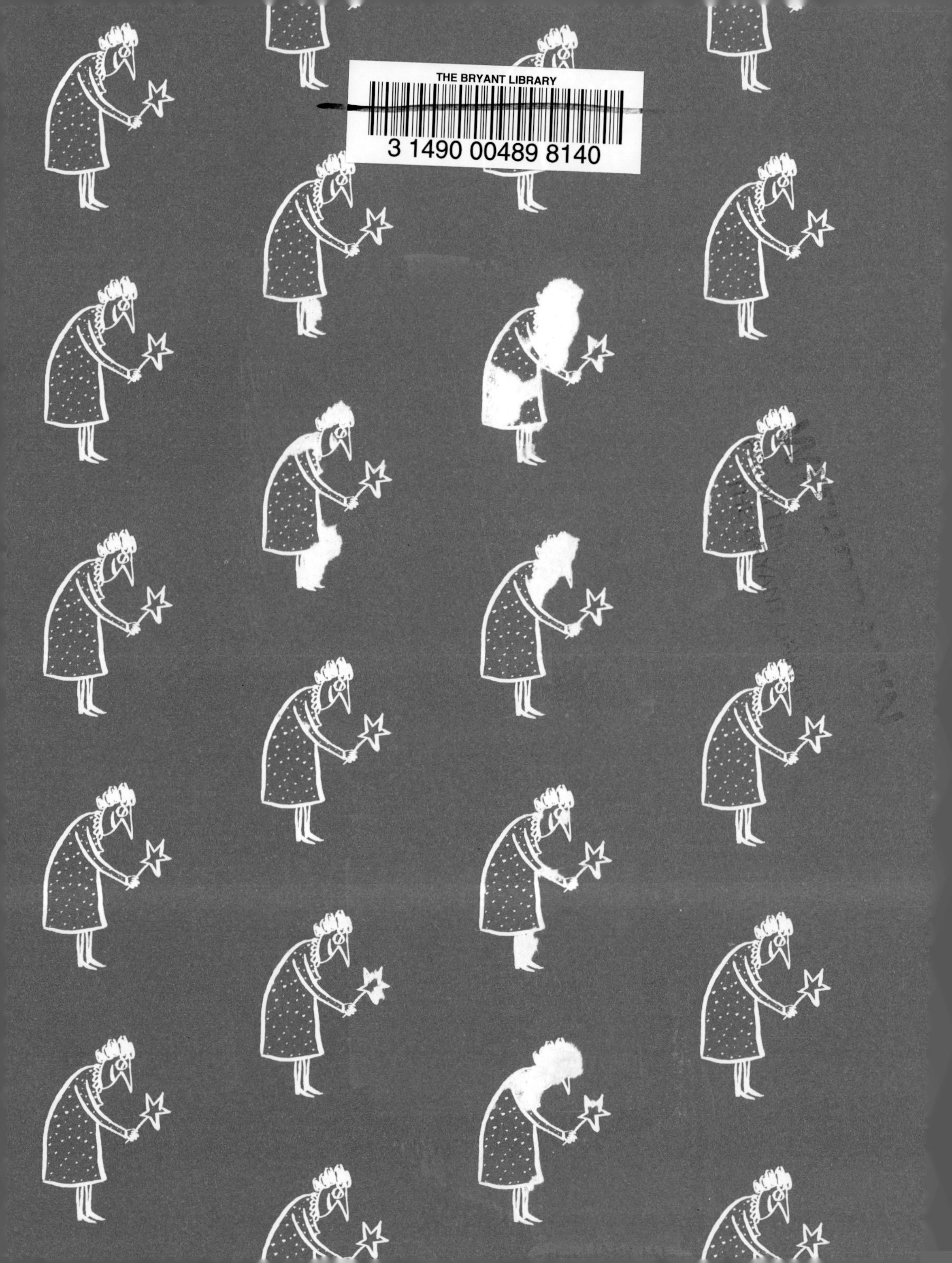